Mastering Martial Arts

A Complete Guide to JUDO

ROBERTO GHETTI

Enslow Publishing
101 W. 23rd Street
Suite 240
New York, NY 10011
USA
enslow.com

Published in 2018 by Enslow Publishing, LLC.
101 W. 23rd Street, Suite 240, New York, NY 10011

Library of Congress Cataloging-in-Publication Data
Names: Ghetti, Roberto, author.
Title: A complete guide to judo / Roberto Ghetti.
Description: New York, NY : Enslow Publishing, 2018. | Series: Mastering Martial Arts | Audience: Grades 7-12 | Includes bibliographical references and index.
Identifiers: LCCN 2017001879 | ISBN 9780766085473 (library bound : alk. paper)
Subjects: LCSH: Judo--Juvenile literature.
Classification: LCC GV1114 .G48 2018 | DDC 796.815/2--dc23
LC record available at https://lccn.loc.gov/2017001879

Printed in the United States of America

To Our Readers: We have done our best to make sure all websites in this book were active and appropriate when we went to press. However, the author and the publisher have no control over and assume no liability for the material available on those websites or on any websites they may link to. Any comments or suggestions can be sent by e-mail to customerservice@enslow.com.

Photo Credits: Cover © Volodymyr Melnyk (Master1305) | Dreamstime

Contents

Introduction

The goal of this book is provide an overview of judo in a simple yet comprehensive way. Judo is a combat discipline and at the same time a sport; it's an excellent educational activity that also provides physical exercise for younger students. To explain more about this sport, we offer comprehensive photos along with specific technical terminology and commentary.

In the table below, you will also find some pronunciation instructions to help you say the Japanese words correctly. These lexical classifications come from the *judo kodokan* method in Tokyo, the Japanese headquarters of judo and the origin of technical judo references for all students worldwide. In addition to reading the instructions in this book, we recommend that the reader join an approved martial arts center and learn from certified teachers to further their skills in the practice and study of judo.

How to Use This Book

According to tradition, the techniques in this book are labeled with their Japanese name with translations provided afterward in parentheses. The translations are not always purely literal, as the true meaning of the names would invariably be lost. The photographs that accompany the descriptions of the techniques will help explain the moves more accurately.

To perform the exercises correctly, *tori* (the person performing the action) and *uke* (the person receiving the action) will first study and try the techniques in a static position, which is easiest.

In the second phase, they will unite the dynamic movements with the execution of the actions, increasing their ability to perform with specific methods of training.

The History of Judo: The Method of Adaptability

The Difference Between Ju Do and Ju Jitsu

Japanese martial arts, including judo, were codified between the nineteenth and twentieth centuries, and their common technical origin is *ju jitsu*. Before delving into the history of judo, it's useful to know the etymology and significance of the terms *ju do* and *ju jitsu*.

Professor Jigoro Kano

The ideogram *ju* corresponds to the concepts of "adaptability," "resilience," and "harmony." It represents the possibility to adapt to circumstances without physical or spiritual resistance, but also includes seizing the opportunity to use the energy and power appointed to us.

For example, think about the image of a bamboo stalk bent on the floor by the enormous power of a storm, and how it stands back up with vigor as the storm passes. Or picture a tree whose branches yield to the ground under the weight of snow but return to their proper, natural position when the sun thaws the ice. These perfectly conceptualize the idea of ju.

The Chinese-Japanese symbol for *do* (or, in Japanese, *michi*) corresponds to the idea of "path," or "method," and refers to the path one needs to travel to discover that to live freely, you must take advantage of the positive aspects of the eternally problematic idea of "choice."

In contrast, the idea of jitsu corresponds to the concepts of "science," "art," and "technique." Jitsu refers to the study and methods of the fight and its military application, which is a form of combat with bare hands or weapons.

Jigoro Kano and the Birth of Judo

Judo was conceived and codified by Professor Jigoro Kano. To understand the evolution of judo around the world, it's helpful to understand a little bit of his life, which was wholly dedicated to the development and proliferation of the discipline throughout the world.

Jigoro Kano was born on October 18, 1860, in Mikage, a small city in the Hyogo district of Japan. He was the third son of Jirosaku Mareshiba Kano, naval attendant for the Tokugawa shogun (the supreme governor of a district, who was appointed directly by the emperor). The title was probably just honorary, and the Kano family's financial success was more likely due to their sake brewery, the Japanese alcohol made from fermented rice.

As a child, Kano was weak, but blessed with a lively intelligence. Other kids nicknamed him *nobe no suke* after a samurai (warrior of high rank), whom he physically resembled. Kano proved himself to be a gifted student, but because of his frailty, he was unable to play many sports and was constantly picked on by stronger classmates.

Kano decided to devote himself to physical conditioning, but the complex Japanese social system in place at the time made it difficult. The traditional, ancient disciplines were not terribly practical for an aspiring athlete, and Western sports had yet to make their way abroad, so it was also difficult to get all the materials necessary for various activities. At long last, Kano was able to find baseball and canoeing equipment, and in 1878, he founded the Kasei Baseball Club, the first Japanese baseball club.

However, despite his efforts he could not improve his strength and athletic abilities as much as he wanted. To achieve his goals, he decided to instead follow a dedicated method of ju jitsu.

This decision was not simple: at this time, the ancient martial art had completely lost its prestige. The decline in popularity was due in part to the introduction of firearms, which had completely changed combat, almost entirely eliminating hand-to-hand fighting and combat using traditional weapons. Furthermore, ju jitsu's lack of popularity was also due to the simple fact that it was *old*.

Many schools had closed due to declining numbers of students, and the students who did stay were regularly pestered by other violent, non-affiliated people, often resulting in fights about money or gambling. Kano's father forbid him from attending these morally decadent schools. However, Jigoro attended a foreign language school and received the basics of ju jitsu secretly from a classmate.

In 1877, Kano matriculated to the Faculty of Arts at the University of Tokyo and finally escaped his father's control. He became part of Hachinosuke Fukuda's school of ju jitsu, who became the first of three great teachers to help the young Kano understand the secrets of the two fundamental schools.

The master Fukuda belonged to the school of *tenschin shinyo ryu*, whose name, literally translated, means "school of the willow heart." The school specialized in *atemi waza* (striking techniques), *osaekomi waza* (immobilizing techniques), and *shime waza* (choking techniques); from its origin we find the fusion of the previous schools, *yoshin ryu* and *shin no shindo ryu*. The Yoshin Ryu was founded by a Japanese doctor who had traveled to China to study and became familiar with Chinese martial arts. He returned to Japan and created a new method of combat, which combined his new knowledge with his medical background.

A member of the Osaka police added new techniques to the school, founding the Shin no Shindo Ryu style, whose system of teaching was especially based in its practice. Following these principles, Fukuda, the *sensei* (teacher) of the Tenshin Shinyo Ryu, showed these techniques to his own students and invited them to continuously perform while giving very few theoretical explanations. Before his death, impressed by young Kano's passion and will to learn, Fukuda gave him the *densho* (the secret texts of the school) as an inheritance.

Kano found a new teacher to continue his way along the path of knowledge—this was Mataemon Iso, the *waka sensei* (young master) under whose guidance Kano learned the secrets of Master Fukuda. Mataemon Iso was gifted with such an extraordinary technical ability that Kano immediately recognized him as having reached a level of perfection unique among all experts.

After Kano received the densho, he was accepted as a student of Iikubo Tsunetoshi, who did not belong to the previous ryu, but who was an expert in another fundamental school, the *kito*. The techniques of his style were very different from those Kano had learned up until that point: they presented the forms of study called the *kata*, whose uniqueness was in the techniques of *nage waza* (protection techniques). The study of the kata was required for students to improve and perfect the execution of moves, and completely replaced armor with the traditional clothing worn in other schools. The densho of Kito Ryu opened the doors to a wider knowledge of techniques for Kano, and the study of the *koshiki no kata* (the model or ancient form) of judo worked to keep the spread of the discipline alive during this epoch.

Given that Jigoro Kano was known as an expert in both ryus, according to imperial legislation, he now had the ability to create a new ryu.

He named this new study *kodokan* ("the point of study

of the way of the method"). Founded in 1882, this would mark the year judo was officially born. The different concept between ju jitsu and the new judo kodokan consisted of the transformation of defensive techniques against a stronger opponent; this method was designed to teach students mutual respect for one another, while simultaneously proceeding toward enlightenment.

Kano considered any financial help from his family an extravagance, and instead survived solely on the limited contributions of his new students. The first kodokan headquarters was a small room in the Eisho Buddhist temple, prepared with twelve *tatami* (the Judo pads measuring 6 feet by 3 feet [about 2 meters by 1 meter] in the West). The official opening in 1882 can be observed by reading the enrollment of the students on the register (signed with blood, following the traditional style) of the kodokan; the first student was Izu, who joined on June 5, 1882. He was seventeen years old and had previously studied under Kano in his ju jitsu course.

The desire to adapt an ancient technique to the new demands of Japanese society was the necessary push to find unprecedented techniques to show new students the possibilities of the discipline.

Kano also had to create a uniform (*judogi*) suitable for the practice. He opted for a white cotton kimono, loose fitting and heavier than the traditional uniform, cut to the hips and tied with a belt (*obi*) of various colors according to the student's level of technical experience (white, brown, and black in Japan and white, yellow, orange, green, blue, brown, and black in the West). The new outfit was finished with long white pants, cut almost to the ankles.

There were nine students in the first year. The second headquarters opened close to the Eisho Temple, with twenty-four tatami. The expansion of the school was rapid thanks to the repeated victories over all the ju jitsu schools that challenged the kodokan in the *dojo yaburi* (practice to challenge a school of martial arts). The rise of popularity continued until 1958, when it moved to its current headquarters, which can accommodate hundreds of judoka on more than 7,000 square feet (650 square meters) of tatami spread through seven rooms.

The first president of kodokan was, of course, Jigoro Kano himself. In 1894 the Council of the Kodokan was founded, and six years after that the *yudansha kai* (Association of the Dan, the levels of black belt) was instituted. In 1949 the Federation of Judo was founded, which absorbed the Association of the Dan and established the central headquarters close to the kodokan.

With the evolution of judo, Jigoro Kano spelled out the most important principles arising from the study of the method in 1921:

- *seiryoku zenyo* (the efficient use of energy)
- *jitakyoei* (prosperity and mutual well-being)

An educator by both vocation and personal conviction, Kano always believed that nothing is more important than education. He brought this idea forward while also maintaining and cultivating the traditions of Japan.

In particular, he contributed to the dissemination of judo and occupied important positions: in 1909 he became the first Japanese member of the International Olympic Committee, and two years later he founded and became the first president of the Athletic Association of Japan. Starting with the 1912 Olympic Games in Stockholm, Kano was the representative for Japan in all subsequent games and IOC reunions. In 1928 he succeeded in making Tokyo the site of the XII Olympics 1940. This was his final act for Japanese athletics: while returning to Japan from Cairo on May 5, 1938, he died from pneumonia on the Hikawa Maru boat.

Judo as an Athletic Discipline

Judo appeared in an international sports competition for the first time in Paris, specifically in the European Championships in 1951. In 1956 the first World Judo Championships was organized in Tokyo, and in the 1964 Olympic Games (also in Tokyo), organizers added a system of weight categories. The creation of weight categories changed the spirit of Jigoro Kano's judo kodokan, but it was a necessary change because, despite using the technical principles, a larger athlete who knows the same techniques will still dominate a smaller opponent. Since then, with the support of the IOC and the International Judo Federation, the number of judo competitions never diminished, but rather increased in either the amount of participants or the different organizations that included the sport in competitions: judo became a sport offered to women in the Olympics, and was featured in the European Championships, the European Team, the World Military Championship, the World Cup for Teams, the World Universities, and the European Club Cup. All of these contrast with the spiritual, ethic, and moral beliefs taught by Jigoro Kano. Judo was not designed for public competitions—it was developed as a method to be applied to every person to train their body and spirit. But if it hadn't been for the dominant force of competition, judo would not have spread in the way that has made the sport so relevant today.

Judo Practice

Place and Equipment

Judo is practiced in a dojo (a place to study the methods), which houses the tatamis. Judo's typical uniform is called a judogi, which is complete with a belt of a specific color according to the *kyu* (level) the student has reached.

The judogi is white, and the kyu are the following in ascending order: white belt, yellow belt, orange belt, green belt, blue belt, brown belt.

There are ten *dan*, or levels, of the black belt that go in ascending order. In principle there is no limit to the number of dan ranks.

CLASSES BY AGE AND WEIGHT CATEGORIES

Pre-Competition	Competition
Children: From six to eight years old. Adolescents: From nine to ten years old. Beginners A: From eleven to twelve years old.	Beginners B: From thirteen to fourteen years old. Cadets: From fifteen to sixteen years old. Juniors: From seventeen to nineteen years old. Seniors: From twenty to thirty-five years old.
Male Weight Categories	**Female Weight Categories**
Beginners: -75, 75–84, 84–93, 93–100, 100–110, 110–120, 120–130, 130–150, 150+ lbs. Cadets: -101, 101–110, 110–121, 121–132, 132–146, 146–161, 161–179, 179+ lbs. Juniors: -132, 132–146, 146–161, 161–179, 179–198, 198–220, 220+ lbs. Seniors: -132, 132–146, 146–161, 161–179, 179–198, 198–220, 220+ lbs.	Beginners: -71, 71–79, 79–88, 88–97, 97–106, 106–115, 115–123, 123–134, 134+ lbs. Cadets: -88, 88–97, 97–106, 106–115, 115–126, 126–139, 139–154, 154+ lbs. Juniors: -106, 106–115, 115–126, 126–139, 139–154, 154–172, 172+ lbs. Seniors: -106, 106–115, 115–126, 126–139, 139–154, 154–172, 172+ lbs.
	Non-Competition
	Thirty years and older: all of those who do not want to or can't compete, and those who have surpassed the age limit for competition.

Training

Training times vary from an hour to an hour and a half twice a week. If an athlete is preparing for a competition, they will train more frequently, and these sessions will last somewhere between an hour and a half and two hours. Training generally develops in this order:

Starting position and greeting in the zarei *form (kneeling)*

1. *Zarei*: The traditional kneeling greeting done at the beginning of class between the students and professor before any training or ground fighting.
2. *Ritsurei*: The traditional upright greeting done before every study session or training fight.

Starting position and greeting in the ritsurei *form (standing)*

3. *Taiso* (warm-up exercises).
4. Study of the *ukemi waza* (holding technique and breaking falls):
   - *ushiro ukemi* (fall backward)
   - *yoko ukemi* (fall sideways, either to the right or left)
   - *mae ukemi* (fall forward)
   - *zempo kaiten ukemi* (jumping and rotating fall forward, right, or left)

Starting position and fall in the ushiro ukemi *form*

5. *Uchikomi* (training to enter the technique), *ya ku soku geiko* (training for opportunities) etc.
6. Study of the *kihon* (fundamentals):

- nage waza (throwing technique)
- osaekomi waza (immobilization technique)
- kansetsu waza (dislocation technique)
- shime waza (choking technique)

Starting position and fall in the yoko ukemi *form*

Starting position and fall in the zempo kaiten ukemi *form*

7. Study of the kata with the advanced knowledge founded in the principle methods of kodokan:

- *nage no kata* (throwing form)
- *katame no kata* (form of hold)
- *kime no kata* (form of decision)
- *ju no kata* (form of adaptability)
- *koshiki no kata* (ancient form)
- *itsutsu no kata* (form of five principles)
- *kodokangoshin jitsu* (form of defense technique)
- *gonosen no kata* (form of counterattacks)

8. *Randori* (generally intense combat-like training with nage waza).

9. *Ne waza* (generally intense, combat-like training using *osaekomi kansetsu* and *shime waza*).

10. *Shiai* (competition accompanied by the upright fighting phases and ground fights with officially sanctioned rules).

11. Zarei (traditional knee salute) done at the end of class between the students and teacher.

Fundamentals

The *shisei* are the positions of the body (natural, defensive, and offensive) that can be adopted during judo practice. There are many positions, but there are two principles most commonly used in execution and open training:

- *shizen hon tai* (fundamental natural body position)
- *jigo hon tai* (fundamental defensive body position)

Above: Migi shizen tai *(right natural position)*
Below: Migi jigo tai *(right defensive position)*

The walking forms are:

- *ayumi ashi* (move the feet normally)
- *tsugui ashi* (slide the feet)

An international rule allows only determined *kumi kata* during competition and excludes all others forms.

Following the technical program, we won't omit any of the defender's forms, not even those barred from competition.

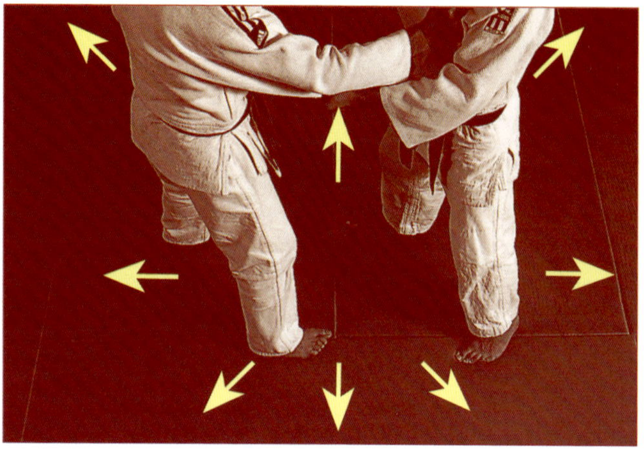

Glie shintai waza *(linear technique displacemet) can be performed in every direction, forward and back.*

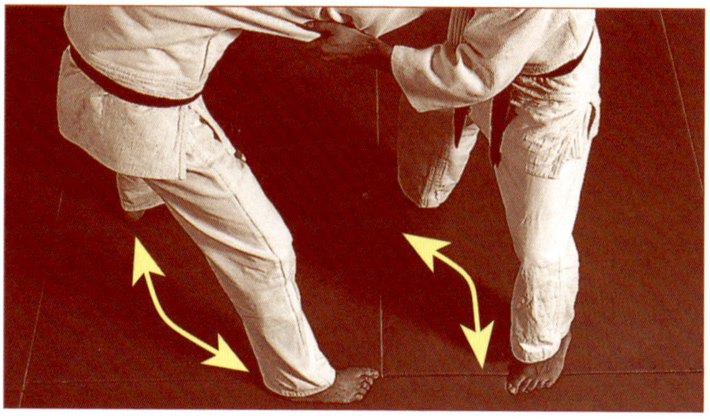

The circular displacement technique is called tai sabaki.

The fundamental forms of grabbing are called the kihon kumi kata. They can be performed by tori (the person who initiates the action):

- In *migui* form (right), the right hand grabs the judogi flap a little below the left clavicle of uke (the person who follows the action and performs the necessary reaction), and grabs uke's right sleeve at the elbow with the left hand;
- In *hidari* (left), tori switches the Migui position. The defender takes the flap of the judogi, which is called *tsurite* (grab above the lapel to pull, lift, and unbalance). The sleeve pull is called *hikite* (grab the sleeve and unbalance your opponent).

The kumi kata can be:

- *ai yotsu* (symmetrical grab between uke and tori, meaning the right guard against the right guard)
- *kenka yotsu* (opposite grab between uke and tori, meaning left against right).

These two forms vary according to the ability of the judoka to perform the diverse techniques, with both controlling the lapels, sleeves, belt, or pants of the judogi.

The kumi kata *(pressure form), of which three examples are illustrated here, allow the student to practice judo techniques.*

Balance and Application Techniques

The fundamental technique of unbalancing your opponent is what allows you to perform judo with maximum effectiveness and minimum force. The potential imbalances connected to a body in space are infinite, like the points of a sphere around that person; there is, however, a conventional classification called *happo no kuzushi*, with eight fundamental directions of imbalance, applicable to the different executions of possible techniques.

Kuzushi

Tsukuri

The phases allowing the techniques of judo to be put into practice are:

- *kuzushi* (corporal imbalance of uke)
- *tsukuri* (preparation of the technical gesture's construction)
- *kake* (application and the execution's final phase)

These three moments happen simultaneously, but the results differ greatly depending upon the student's comprehension and experience. There are multiple methods for success, but the following are used the most:

Kake

- *tobi komi* (jump inward)
- *mawari komi* (rotate inward)
- *hikidashi* (static pull)
- *sutemi* (sacrifice one's own balance)

Note: In the text the description of kuzushi will always refer to uke's body.

Nage Waza: Throwing Techniques

The technical classification of the nage waza presented in the text is from the kodokan method of Tokyo, and was modified multiple times since 1895. Its current form was established in 1997.

The nage waza is part of the subdivision of technical throwing movements, which are divided into:

- *tachi waza* (throwing techniques from standing position), which in turn is divided into three groups that specify the parts of the body used in whatever mode preferred by the tori while using the technique
- *te waza* (the group of techniques using the arms to perform the throws)
- *koshi waza* (the group of techniques using the hips to perform the throws)
- *ashi waza* (the group of techniques using the legs to perform the throws)
- *sutemi waza* (a throwing technique which sacrifices your own balance), which in turn is divided into two groups that specify the parts of the tori's body that rest on the tatami when they perform the throw:
  - *ma sutemi waza* (the group of techniques which sacrifice your own balance, making you land on your back in the fall)
  - *yoko sutemi waza* (the group of techniques which sacrifice your own balance, making you land on your hips to break the fall)

All of the nage waza techniques can be performed in a right- or left-hand position; thus, all of the sequences in the photographs can be repeated by students in a manner most suitable for any given situation.

The *nage no kata* form part of the nage waza techniques. The former are highlighted with an asterisk (*).

Tachi Waza

First Group: Te Waza

IPPON SEOI NAGE* (One Arm Shoulder Throw)

1. Tori is in front of uke to the right, using a basic hold to the right to displace uke going forward and to the right with the hikite hold; tori places the right foot centrally, respective of uke's feet.

2. Always maintaining traction, tori puts the right arm below uke's right armpit and completes the *tai sabaki*, rotating the left foot backward.

3. To throw, tori lifts uke using the legs and applying force, and continues with the right shoulder toward the left foot.

With the same type of preparation, tori can perform *morote* (with two hands) *seoi nage*, putting the right elbow below uke's right armpit.

Tori can also perform *eri* (with the lapel) *seoi nage*, taking the right part of uke's lapel with the right hand, using four fingers inside and the thumb outside.

SEOI OTOSHI (Over the Shoulder Throw)

1. Tori is situated against uke in a natural position to the right with the basic hold to the right, displacing uke's balance forward and to the right with the hikite hold; in turn, tori moves the right foot backward, rotating the shoulder and maintaining the hold. Tori puts the right elbow below uke's right armpit.

2. Afterward, tori lowers the right knee down to the tatami, using a strong pull forward and throwing uke.

TAI OTOSHI (Body Drop)

1. Tori is situated behind uke to the right, using a basic hold to the right to displace uke's balance forward and to the right with the hikite hold; simultaneously, tori brings the left foot back, rotating the shoulder while keeping a strong hold. Tori puts the right elbow against uke's left side.

2. Tori continues the pull with the left arm and uke's left side with the right elbow; rotating backward, tori places the right foot with external support toward uke's right side and throws uke.

KATA GURUMA* (Shoulder Wheel)

1. Tori is behind uke to the right, using a basic hold to the right to displace uke's balance forward and to the right with the hikite hold; tori simultaneously brings the left foot back, turns the shoulder, and crouches into jigo hon tai position.

2. Tori continues the pull with the hikite hold and, with the right hand, holds uke's right leg and forces the support of uke's abdomen against tori's shoulders.

3. Now tori uses the arm to continue pulling, furthering the rotation over the shoulders and throwing uke.

UKI OTOSHI* (Floating Drop)

1. Tori is behind uke to the right, using a basic hold to the right and taking a step back with the right foot.

2. Tori retreats with the left foot, greatly lengthening the support backward and displacing uke's balance forward and to the right with the hikite hold.

3. Tori keeps forcefully pulling with both holds toward the left hip, forcing uke to fall.

UKI OTOSHI (Second Type)

1. Uke attacks with *osotogari* (see page 58).

2. Tori moves the right leg backward and performs a strong pull with the arms toward the same right hip to break uke's balance, throwing uke.

SUMI OTOSHI (Corner Drop)

1. Tori is behind uke to the right. Tori uses a fundamental grab to the right with the right foot.

2. Tori retreats afterward with the left foot, lengthening the support backward; taking a step, tori changes direction, moving in front diagonally and to the right, unbalancing uke with a strong arm rotation downward with the tsurite hold and upward with the hikite hold.

3. Tori continues to forcefully pull and rotates backward (diagonally toward his own right side) and throws uke with both hands.

SUKUI NAGI (Scoop Throw)

1. Uke is in front of tori in a position to the left; tori is in the *mori jigo tai* position and performs the fundamental left hold.

2. Tori takes a step backward, sliding the right foot back from uke's left, and applies the hikite hold, passing the right arm forward.

3. Levering uke with the right leg and performing a strong pull backward toward tori's own right side, tori throws uke.

SUKUI NAGE/ TE GURUMA (Roll with the Hand)

1. This is another way to perform the version of *sukui nage* practiced in the West. Against uke's attack (of koshi waza, *uchi mata,* or O Soto Gari), tori defends, bringing the right foot backward, bending down, and pulling uke's right leg with the left hand.

2. Tori forcefully pushes uke with two arms and separates the legs. Tori lifts uke, with the abdomen taking on some of the effort.

3. With the holds on the lapel, tori turns downward and to the right and, with the leg up and to the left, throws uke over tori's back.

OBI OTOSHI (Belt Drop)

The performance is substantially the same as sukui nage; although it differs as tori grabs uke's belt. The belt is then forcefully pulled forward, with the opposite movement pushing the arm into uke's abdomen.

MOROTE GARI (Takedown with Two Hands)

1. Tori and uke face each other in the natural left position; they have not grasped the basic hold yet.

2. While uke searches for a way to achieve the hold, tori anticipates and, moving forward with the right foot, lowers the body forward. Tori supports the right shoulder on uke's abdomen, putting the head on the right hip while grabbing the knees from behind.

3. Tori applies a strong pressure with the shoulder and a decisive push with the arms. This breaks uke's balance and forces uke to fall on his back.

KUCHIKI DAOSHI (Dead Tree Drop)

1. Tori and uke face each other in a natural right position with the basic hold from the right.

2. Tori, moving the left foot toward the outside of uke's right foot, bends down and, with the hikite hold, unbalances uke with a strong pull to the left and downward. With the right hand, tori grasps the inside of uke's right thigh and pulls forcefully.

3. Tori continues the pull with the left hold moving downward, uniting the right one that pulls the right leg of uke upward. This breaks uke's balance and forces uke to fall backward on his back.

KIBISU GAESHI (Takedown with Heel Pull)

1. Tori and uke face each other in a natural left position, using the basic right hold.

2. Uke moves the right foot forward; tori takes a sliding step backward and keeps his weight on the front left foot. Afterward, tori supports the right knee on the floor with the right hand holding uke's right heel, then pulls forcefully downward and to the right with the hikite hold.

3. With the right hand, tori pulls uke's heel from behind and continues by pushing downward with the left hold, forcing uke to fall.

KOUCHI GAESHI/ KO UCHI GAESHI (Counterattack Against Kouchi Gari)

1. Tori and uke face each other in a natural right position with the basic right hold. Uke performs an attack using kouchi gari (see page 70). Tori, moving his weight to the left foot, avoids the sweep by lifting the right foot.

2. Uke is put off-balance when no contact is made during the sweep; tori takes advantage of this by supporting the right foot to the right and accentuating uke's loss of balance by rotating and pulling the hold to uke's left.

3. Tori continues with the rotating pull with both holds going downward, forcing uke to fall.

UCHI MATA SUKASHI (Evasion from Uchi Mata)

1. Tori and uke face each other in a natural right position, with the basic right hold. Uke performs an attack using uchi mata (see page 66). Tori moves his weight onto the right foot and lifts the left leg, avoiding uke's right leg sweep.

2. Uke is put off-balance due to tori missing the sweep. Tori takes advantage of this and accentuates uke's loss of balance with a rotating push forward with the hold, throwing uke.

YAMA ARASHI (Mountain Storm)

This technique is not allowed in competition.

1. Tori and uke face each other in a natural right position, using the basic right hold. Tori changes the position of the tsurite hold with the thumb on the inside pulling the right side of uke's lapel from the inside downward. Tori performs a strong kuzushi with the hikite hold forward and to the right.

2. Then, with tai sabaki, tori brings the left leg backward and rotates the shoulders and hips to the left. With both holds tori continues to pull right and forward in this position and places the right foot over uke's right ankle.

3. Tori continues the pull with the arms and pushes with the right foot on uke's right ankle, sweeping it and throwing uke.

Second Group: Koshi Waza

OH GOSHI/ O GOSHI (Large Hip Throw)

1. Tori and uke face each other in a natural right position with the basic right hold; tori moves the right foot forward, centered between uke's feet, and unbalances uke forward and to the right. With the palm of the right hand, tori holds uke's back, pulling it forcefully.

2. Now tori brings the left foot back until it's in line with the right foot. Crouching over the legs, tori puts his back on uke's abdomen, strengthening the forward pull.

3. Tori separates the legs to lift uke and continues the pull with the hold, throwing uke.

UKI GOSHI* (Floating Hip Technique)

1. The same preparation as O Goshi (see page 39), but uke resists kuzushi.

2. Consequently, tori does not complete the tai sabaki and stays with the feet parallel, bending the legs and supporting uke's abdomen on the right side.

3. Now tori accentuates the push with the arms, causing uke's body to roll over tori's hips, throwing uke.

TSURI GOSHI (Lifting Hip Throw)

The preparation is the same as for O Goshi (see page 39), but in this case tori holds on to the belt at the back; tori strengthens this hold with kuzushi or kake. Note: When the arm passes below uke's arm the technique is called *ko tsuri goshi;* when it passes inside, it is called *otsuri goshi.*

TSURIKOMI GOSHI/TSURI KOMI GOSHI* (Lifting Pulling Hip Throw)

1. The two opponents face each other in a natural right position, with the basic right hold centered between uke's feet, and tori unbalances uke forward and to the right.

2. Tori brings the left foot backward with a rotation until it's at the same level as the right; squatting slightly over the knees, tori places his back to uke's abdomen, continuing the forward pull. Tori places the right elbow on uke's left side.

3. Tensing the left to lift uke, tori continues the pull with the hold and throws uke.

SODE TSURIKOMI GOSHI/ SODE TSURI KOMI GOSHI (Lifting and Throwing Hip Technique with Elbow)

This is a technique related to *tsurikomi goshi* or, more precisely, a variation in which tori performs the grasp with two hands or *hidari kimi kata*. Tori follows with the technique on the right.

KOSHI GURUMA (Hip Roll)

1. Tori and uke face each other in a natural left position, with the basic left hold and uke in *kenka yotsu*. Tori moves the left foot forward, centering it between uke's feet and throwing uke off-balance left and forward; tori places the left arm on uke's back.

2. After, tori brings the right foot back with a rotation until it's at the same level as the left foot; squatting down, tori places his back to uke's abdomen, moving the hips far out and continuing to pull forward.

3. Then, stretching the legs to lift uke, tori continues pulling with the hold. Supporting uke on his hips, tori throws uke.

HARAI GOSHI* (Hip Sweep)

1. Tori and uke face each other in a natural right position, with the basic right hold. Uke lifts the right foot backward; tori moves the right foot forward in *tsugi ashi*, centering it between uke's legs and unbalancing uke forward and to the right.

2. Now tori retreats by rotating the left foot and placing it on the same level as the right; squatting over the left leg, tori brings the right hip to uke's abdomen, always maintaining the pull forward.

3. At this time, tori uses the right hip to lift uke and the right leg to sweep uke's right leg and throw uke to the ground.

HANE GOSHI (Lifted Hip Technique)

1. Tori and uke face each other in a natural right position, with the basic right hold.

2. Uke brings the right foot back while tori moves the left foot forward in ayumi ashi; tori centers between uke's feet, bends over the left leg, and unbalances uke forward and to the right.

3. Tori follows uke's movement backward and slides the slightly bent right leg together with uke's right leg; after turning the shoulders down and to the left, tori throws uke.

UTSURI GOSHI (Hip Movement)

1. On uke's attack (generally koshi waza), tori defends, lowering the center of gravity and circling uke's waist with the left arm.

2. Having uke supported with the arms, tori lifts uke, stretching the legs and using the abdomen for support.

3. While maintaining this hold and before uke falls, tori moves the left foot forward, and continues by placing uke's abdomen on his left hip and throwing uke over his back.

USHIRO GOSHI (Rear Hip Throw)

1. On uke's attack (generally koshi waza), tori defends by lowering his center of gravity and using the left arm to hug uke's body around the waist.

2. With uke supported with the arm, tori stretches the legs and, using the abdomen, lifts uke.

3. Keeping the hold, tori moves the left foot back when uke falls, throwing uke over his back.

DAKI AGE (High Lift)

1. This technique interrupts the *katame waza* action. Uke has his back on the ground and attacks tori with a choking or dislocation technique; tori passes the arms below the opponent's arms and holds uke by the waist.

2. Placing the feet very close to uke's sides, tori lifts uke.

This execution finishes at this point and tori repositions uke with the back on the tatami, controlling the movement. If this technique is poorly executed, it can cause trauma to the vertebrae and have serious consequences.

Third Group: Ashi Waza

HIZA GURUMA (Throw Over the Knee)

1. Tori and uke face each other in the natural right position with the basic right hold. Tori lifts the right foot back and places it slightly separate from his right, forcing uke to move forward with the left foot.

2. Anticipating uke's right step forward, tori places the left foot on uke's right knee, blocking the movement and forcefully pulling forward.

3. Tori continues the pull with both arms, moving the action in a circular direction and maintaining the block on uke's knee until uke falls.

SASAE TSURIKOMI ASHI/ SASAE TSURI KOMI ASHI* (Pulling and Lifting Foot Block)

Tori and uke face each other in a natural right position, with the fundamental right hold. Like the previous exercise, tori brings the right foot back, slightly separated from the right, forcing uke to move forward with the left foot. Anticipating uke's right step forward, tori now places the left foot on the instep of the right foot, blocking the movement and initiating a strong pull forward and up. Tori continues pulling with both arms, moving in a circular direction. Tori holds uke's foot up with his own foot until uke falls.

HARAI TSURIKOMI ASHI (Lifting and Pulling Leg Sweep)

1. Tori and uke face each other in a natural right position with the basic right hold. Uke holds the right foot back and tori follows the action.

2. Increasing the speed of the action, tori sweeps uke's right foot at the ankle with the sole of his left foot diagonally to the right. When done together with the two holds, this will lift uke.

3. Tori continues the pull and lift with two arms, completing the throw.

DEASHI HARAI/ DE ASHI BARAI (Advancing Foot Sweep)

1. Tori and uke face each other in a natural right position, using the basic right hold. Uke moves forward with the left foot, while tori maintains the position.

2. Uke moves forward with the left foot and tori retreats with the right foot, creating a space to sweep uke's right foot with the left, fearlessly crossing the legs.

3. Anticipating uke's right foot support, tori throws the sweep with the sole of the left foot to uke's right and pulls the hold downward.

OKURI ASHI ARAI/ OKURI ASHI ARAI* (Following Foot Sweep)

1. Tori and uke face each other in the natural right position, with the basic right hold. Tori performs a lateral move to the right and uke follows.

2. Calculating the exact moment of uke's movement, tori sweeps the right foot with his left foot, unbalancing uke and throwing uke over uke's right side.

TSUBAME GAESHI (Swallowtail Counter)

1. Tori reacts to uke's attack in *deashi harai*. Uke sweeps tori's left foot with the right foot and elevates it.

2. With a circular movement of the left leg, tori takes advantage of uke's unbalance, sweeping the right foot with the left and throwing uke.

KOSOTO GARI/ KO SOTO GARI (Small Outside Sweep)

1. Tori and uke face each other in a natural right position, with the basic right hold. Tori moves the left foot forward and places it on the outside of uke's right; tori continues and unbalances uke with a pull to the right.

2. At the same time, tori joins the feet and increases the pull to the right, sweeping with the sole of the left foot to the back part of uke's right foot to throw uke.

KOSOTO GAKE/ KO SOTO GAKE (Small Outside Hook)

1. Tori and uke face each other in a natural right direction, with the basic right hold. Uke moves the left foot forward, while tori stays in position.

2. When uke moves the right foot forward, tori takes their right foot back and, quickly changing direction, unbalances uke backward. Now tori hooks the right foot with his right and continues the action, throwing uke completely backward.

OH SOTO GARI/ O SOTO GARI (Large Outside Sweep)

1. Tori and uke face each other in a natural right position, with the basic right hold.

2. Tori moves the left foot forward, places it alongside uke's right foot, and unbalances uke to uke's right.

3. Now tori quickly throws the right leg forward, keeping the point of the foot down.

4. Tori sweeps uke's right leg with his right leg, throwing uke.

OH SOTO OTOSHI/ O SOTO OTOSHI (Large Outside Drop)

1. Tori and uke face each other in a natural right position with the basic right hold. Tori hooks uke's right leg with his own right and unbalances uke down and to the right.

2. Uke resists the action and increases the push, which puts tori in contact with uke's chest.

3. Tori, sliding the right leg down, supports the front part of the foot on the tatami and moves forward with the left leg, increasing uke's backward unbalance.

4. Continuing the action downward with both arms and pushing with the right leg, tori throws uke.

OH SOTO GURUMA/ O SOTO GURUMA (Large Outside Rotation)

1. The preparation is identical to O Soto Gari, but in this case uke resists the right leg's push.

2. Tori then pushes again, keeping the position but sweeping both of uke's legs.

OH SOTO GAESHI/ O SOTO GAESHI (Large Outside Counterattack)

1. After uke's O Soto Gari attack, tori resists the push.

2. Tori suddenly transfers his weight to the left leg and, moving the support to the left foot, turns 90° to the left, following with *osoto gaeshi.*

OH GURUMA/O GURUMA (Large Rotation)

1. Tori and uke face each other in a natural right position, with the basic right hold. Tori brings the left foot forward and places it, with the point to the left to assist the following rotation, in front of uke's left foot.

2. Tori, rotating completely to the left, places the right leg in front of uke's abdomen, blocking any possible movement forward. At the same time, tori begins to push with the tsurite hold and pulls with hikite.

3. Now tori continues the push and pull with the two arms, giving the action a circular direction and keeping the obstacle (the right leg) in front of uke's abdomen. This will eventually lead to uke losing his balance forward, rotating over tori's right leg, and being thrown.

ASHI GURUMA (Leg Wheel)

1. Tori and uke face each other, the first in a natural left position, the second in natural right position, with both using the basic right hold.

2. Tori moves the left foot forward and places it, with the point to the right to assist with the following hip rotation, centered with respect to uke's feet.

3. Tori unbalances uke forward and to the left by pulling the two holds, bringing the right foot back in tai sabaki, and putting the left leg crosswise in front of uke's left leg. The heel is placed at ankle height to impede the slide to the left, which would allow uke to recover his balance. The left hip does not touch uke's abdomen. Now tori puts more force on the hold to accentuate uke's body rotation and, continuing with the left leg, blocks with his own right leg and performs the throw.

UCHIMATA/ UCHI MATA* (Inner Thigh Throw)

1. Tori and uke face each other, the first in a natural right position with the basic right hold (the tsurite), and the second in a defensive position with the feet parallel. Tori unbalances uke forward.

2. Tori brings the right foot forward and places it centrally in front of uke's right foot. Now tori performs a tai sabaki with the left foot, supporting it in a way that's centered in respect to uke's foot. Tori simultaneously turns the core, with the right leg initiating the sweeping move.

3. Tori continues to push and pull with both arms, performing a circular action and swiping uke's inner left thigh with the right leg, causing uke to fall on his back.

Some forms of uchi mata are considered *koshi waza*, that is, the swipe is performed at uke's inner right thigh with tori's right hip as the point of support.

UCHI MATA GAESHI, HANE GOSHI GAESHI, HARAI GOSHI GAESHI (Counterattack Against Uchi Mata, Hane Goshi, Harai Goshi)

Tori uses one of the prepared techniques against uke's attack. Tori hooks uke's left foot with his left foot (generally the supporting foot). Swiping uke's foot and pushing in the opposite direction, tori throws uke.

OH UCHI GARI/ O UCHI GARI (Large Inside Sweep)

1. Tori and uke face each other, tori in the natural right position with the basic right hold, and uke in *migi kumi kata* and *hidari shizen tai*. Tori brings the right foot forward and centers it between uke's feet; now tori begins the kuzushi phase back and to the left, while sliding the left leg backward to the right.

2. Continuing this unbalancing action, tori hooks uke's left leg at the calf with his right.

3. Prolonging the push with two arms, tori steps with the right leg in a circular direction, which swipes uke's left leg inward and forces uke to fall on his back.

OH UCHI GAESHI/ O UCHI GAESHI (Counterattack Against O Uchi Gari)

Against uke's *o uchi gari*, tori unbalances uke in the same direction, back and to the left, and uses the same leg that uke used to swipe—the left—to hook and swipe uke's right and throw him onto his back. Tori can perform a swipe on uke's left or right leg.

KOUCHI GARI/ KO UCHI GARI (Small Inside Sweep)

1. Tori and uke face each other in a natural right position, with the basic right hold.

2. Tori moves the right foot forward and places it in front, centering it with respect to uke's feet. Now tori begins the kuzushi phase downward and to the left. After sliding the left foot back and to the right, tori brings the sole of the right foot to uke's right heel with a circular cutting movement.

3. Tori continues the push with both arms and, with the action of the right foot, cuts uke's right heel inwardly, causing uke to fall on his back.

Sutemi Waza

Fourth Group: Ma Sutemi Waza

TOMOE NAGE* (Circle Throw)

1. Tori and uke face each other with the basic right hold. Uke pushes forward and tori resists at first. After tori brings the left foot backward and places it centrally respective of uke's feet, tori gives into the push.

2. Tori goes to sit as close to his left heel as possible, and, bending the legs, supports the right foot on the lower part of uke's abdomen, pulling uke forward with two arms and accentuating this with uke's Kuzushi move.

3. When on the floor, tori stretches the leg and pushes with the right foot upward, sustaining uke's weight and continuing the movement of the pull with both arms. This results in uke being thrown over tori's head and onto his back.

URA NAGE* (Rear Throw)

1. This technique is frequently used as a counterattack. Uke performs an attack, tori stoops to defend himself and, with the left arm, rolls uke's body at the hip, maintaining the right hand's hold on the lapel.

2. Tori stretches the legs, grasping uke forcefully with the arms and pushing with the abdomen upward, lifting uke. When uke is lifted, tori leans backward until the back is on the ground and throws uke behind himself onto uke's back.

SUMI GAESHI* (Corner Throw)

1. Tori and uke face each other with the basic right hold in the migi jigo tai position; the two perform a backward pull.

2. Tori moves the left foot forward, centrally respective of uke's feet, and continues the pull with both arms, placing the right foot below the left leg, close to the knee. Now tori sits as close as possible to uke's left heel.

3. Tori continues the backward movement, and when he's on his back, stretches the leg, pushing with the instep of the right foot upward, and continuing the pulling movement with both arms. This combined action results in tori throwing uke backward over tori's own head.

HIKIKOMI GAESHI (Takedown to the Ground)

The action is the same as the *sumi gaeshi*, but in this case with the hold on the belt. In the West it's defined as *obi tori gaeshi* (the one who grabs the belt and takes down).

UDE HISHIGI TE GATAME (Hand Lock Arm Break)

1. In judo there are multiple actions that are improperly called *hikomi gaeshi*, and which function not so much to achieve points, but more for moving combat from the feet down to the floor. These techniques are described as "drag downs." Some of them have a denomination, and others don't—*ude hishigi te gatame* is one example. Tori performs a left-handed hold on uke's left lapel, passing below uke's right arm. Uke takes a right hold on tori's left lapel, which supports the wrist with the right hand.

2. Tori turns with a jump to the left, using the right leg and making a lever out of uke's right arm.

3. Due to the arm disclocation, uke is forced to fall forward onto his back.

TAWARA GAESHI (Rice Bag Throw)

1. Generally this is used by uke against the *morote gari* attack (see page 32). Tori lengthens the left leg backward to resist the attack and supports uke's body with both arms.

2. Before moving backward, tori should unbalance uke until kuzushi is made evident, with at least a one-foot distance from the tatami.

3. Now tori can complete the action and throw uke.

Fifth Group: Yoko Sutemi Waza

UKI WAZA* (Floating Drop Throw)

1. Tori and uke face each other with the basic right hold. Uke moves the right foot forward.

2. Against uke's step, tori lengthens the left leg in front of uke's right foot and sits as close as possible to tori's right heel, keeping the left leg stretched and the left foot pointed. Simultaneously, tori strongly pulls with two holds downward and to the right.

3. Once tori is on the side, tori continues the pull with both arms; the throw is over uke's back in a left and diagonal direction from tori.

YOKO OTOSHI (Side Drop Throw)

1. Tori and uke face each other with the basic right hold. Uke moves sideways with the right foot and tori performs a strong pull with two holds at the right, creating the kuzushi.

2. Tori sits as close as possible to his right heel. Tori lengthens the right leg against uke's step until, with a pointed foot, they stretch it to the side of uke's right foot. Tori continues the pull with both arms, finally forcing uke to fall.

TANI OTOSHI (Valley Drop)

1. Generally performed like kaeshi waza (counterattack technique), *tani otoshi* can, however, function as its own technique. Uke attacks and tori defends, lowering the center of gravity and moving the right foot toward the right while simultaneously grabbing uke's body.

2. Now tori lengthens the left leg behind uke's legs and throws uke backward.

YOKO WAKARE (Side Separation)

1. Tori and uke face each other with the basic right hold. Tori takes the initiative and performs a pull forward and to the right with the arms, taking a step to the left with the right leg and supporting it in front of uke's right leg.

2. After the first step, tori lengthens the left leg forward, sitting as close as possible to his right heel and keeping the left leg extended and the left foot pointed. With his own body, tori makes an obstacle and simultaneously performs a strong pull forward and to the right with the two holds, throwing uke.

YOKO GAKE* (Side Drop)

1. Tori and uke face each other, with the basic right hold in *migi shizen tai*. Tori begins to unbalance uke to the right and presses the sole of the left foot on uke's right ankle.

2. Impeding uke's ability to recover his balance and sliding the right foot, tori increases the pull of the arms to the right and, always maintaining the hook on uke's foot, throws uke to the side onto the tatami.

DAKI WAKARE (High Separation)

1. Uke is on all fours; tori clings to uke's body with the arms, holding slightly above the right side.

2. Forcefully turning to the right and keeping contact with uke, tori throws uke onto uke's back, finishing with a rotation on the left side.

YOKO GURUMA* (Side Wheel)

1. This technique is performed like *kaeshi waza*, as seen below, or as its own technique. Against uke's attack, tori defends by lowering the center of gravity, sliding the right foot forward, and grabbing uke's body with his arms.

2. In this moment, tori performs a forward rotation with his entire body, grabbing uke's right leg between tori's feet. Now tori supports himself on his left side and, keeping the hold with two arms, throws uke over his back.

SOTO MAKIKOMI (Outer Wrap Throw)

1. Tori and uke face each other with the basic right hold in *migi shizen tai*. Tori brings the right foot forward and places it in front, centered in respect to uke's feet. Tori begins a pull for kuzushi forward and to the right.

2. At this point, tori performs Tai Sabaki with the left foot backward and prepares the tsurite hold, turning with the hips in front of uke's body, while tori's right arm controls uke's right arm.

3. Tori extends the right arm outward and, turning with purpose, throws uke to the ground.

UCHI MAKIKOMI (Inner Wraparound Throw)

The *makikomi* form can be applied as the final phase as well as with other throwing techniques. Starting from *ippon seoi nage* (see page 22), tori releases the body and places the left foot behind uke's right foot. Continuing the rotation, tori supports the right knee on the tatami and throws uke.

HANE MAKIKOMI (Jumping Wraparound Throw)

Tori makes a *hane goshi* (see pg 46); uke resists. Afterward, tori, letting go of the tsurite hold, proceeds to tumble.

HARAI MAKIKOMI (Wraparound Hip Sweep)

Tori performs *harai goshi* (see page 45); uke resists. Tori, letting go of the tsurite hold, proceeds to tumble.

UCHI MATA MAKIKOMI (Inner Thigh Wraparound)

Tori performs *uchi mata* (see page 66); uke resists. Tori, letting go of the tsurite hold, continues the tumble.

O SOTO MAKIKOMI (Large Outer Wraparound Throw)

Tori performs O Soto Gari (see page 58); uke resists. Tori, letting go of the tsurite hold, continues the tumble.

KANI BASAMI (Flying Scissors Throw)

This technique is not allowed in competition.

1. Tori supports the top part of uke's lapel with the right hand and places the other hand on uke's left sleeve; uke has the right leg forward, tori the left.

2. Tori lifts the right leg crosswise in front of uke's abdomen.

3. Suddenly, while still maintaining the pull, tori brings the left leg behind uke's left leg and, with a pinching move (the right leg pushes backward and the left leg pushes forward), throws uke.

KAWAZU GAKE (Modified Hook)

Tori hooks uke's leg by wrapping it in tori's own; in competition this technical movement is allowed to oppose an attack from uke (*ushiro goshi,* O Soto Gari, *ura nage*; see pages 48, 58, and 72). In the *kawazu gake,* codified as KDK, the throw is produced by tori lifting his own leg, which is hooked to uke's, and making a swipe in the opposite direction of tori's knee joint.

This technique is not allowed in competition if used to throw. It is only allowed as a defensive technique.

Katame Waza: Holding Techniques

The technical classification of katame waza presented here is the one from the judo kodokan method of Tokyo, which we discussed earlier.

The katame waza is part of the subdivision of holding techniques that form part of the ground fights. They are divided into various parts:

- *osae waza* (immobilization techniques)
- *shime waza* (choking techniques)
- *kansetsu waza* (joint techniques)

All of the katame waza techniques can be performed on the right or left side; thus, in performing the reverse form, all of the sequences in the photographs can be repeated by students in the manner most suitable for each situation.

These form part of the katame waza techniques which also comprise the *katame no kata*; these are noted with an asterisk (*).

First Group: Osaekomi Waza

HON KESA GATAME (Basic Cross Hold)

Tori sits at uke's side and grab's uke's lapel and uke's right arm with the left hand. Tori's legs are separated and the feet are supported on the tatami; the majority of the pressure is on uke's right shoulder, head, and neck.

KUZURE KESA GATAME* (Variation of the Basic Cross Hold)

The starting position is the same as *hon kesa gatame*. While tori's right arm is placed below uke's left armpit, and the hand is behind the neck, tori grabs uke's lapel. Differing from the previous technique, the pressure is focused more on uke's chest.

MAKURA KESA GATAME (Mat Hold)

All of the variations of *kesa gatame* are defined as *kuzure*; however, we have a different classification in the West. For example, in *makura kesa gatame*, tori is seated closer to uke's right shoulder, with the right side next to uke's head, which is held under the right thigh. Tori controls uke's left arm, clutching the back part of the right knee with the right hand.

USHIRO KESA GATAME (Inner Cross Hold)

1. Tori is placed opposite to uke's body but with the same control approached from the previous exercise. With the right hand holding uke's belt and the left arm in front of uke's abdomen, tori controls uke's left arm.

2. Another variation is that tori is beside uke and controls uke's left arm, which passes behind the back, held at the wrist and under the left armpit.

KATA GATAME* (Shoulder Hold)

Tori is positioned with the right knee beside uke and the left leg extended, pushing away; the right arm passes below uke's neck and the right hand grabs the left; closing the inside of the hold on uke's neck and right arm.

KAMI SHIHO GATAME* (Four-Corner Top Hold)

Tori is behind uke's head, supporting uke's chest and slipping the arms under uke's shoulders. The hand holds uke's belt, while the feet are pointed downward; tori pushes forward, regardless of whether the legs are bent or straight.

KUZURE KAMI SHIHO GATAME* (Variation of the Four-Corner Top Hold)

In this variation, tori's position is slightly diagonal and the right arm passes below uke's right armpit. Four fingers of the right hand hold the inner part of the judogi's lapel.

YOKO SHIHO GATAME* (Four-Corner Side Hold)

Tori is situated beside uke and supports the chest above his own; the right arm passes between uke's legs and holds the belt, while the left passes below the neck and holds the judogi; the legs, whether bent or straight, are always pushing.

TATE SHIHO GATAME (Four-Corner Vertical Hold)

Tori rides on the inside of uke and controls uke's head, while the right shoulder and the right arm pass through the right arm below uke's neck and clutches the left hand; the feet are below uke's thighs.

Second Group: Shime Waza

NAMI JUJI JIME (Natural Cross Choke)

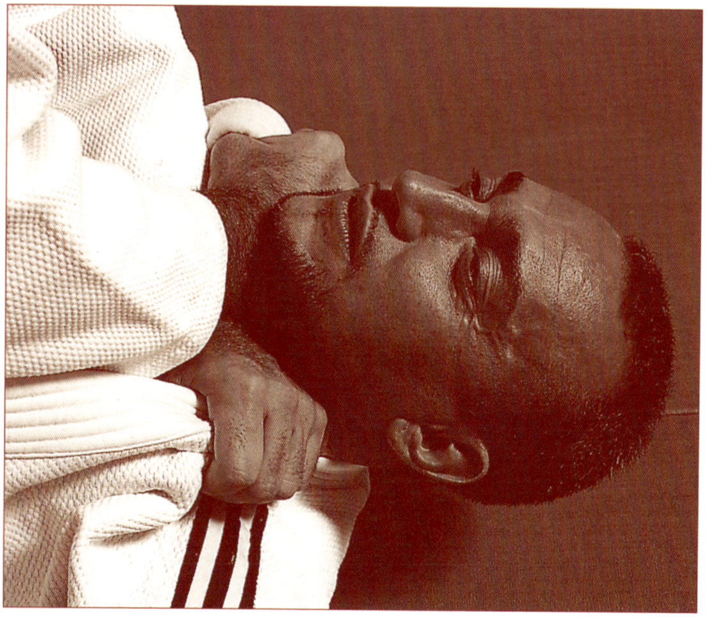

Given the great possibility of injury, a student should use choking techniques with extreme caution.

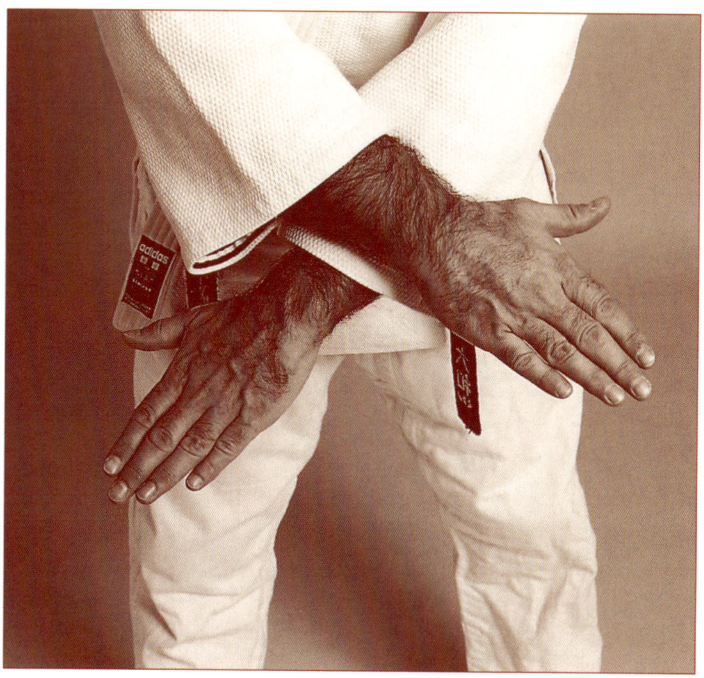

The pressure is applied laterally on uke's neck with the pinkie (the hands are crossed as shown in the image).

GYAKU JUJI JIME* (Reverse Cross Choke)

In this case the pressure is also applied laterally to uke's neck, but with the thumb (the hands are crossed in the inverse position as shown in the image below).

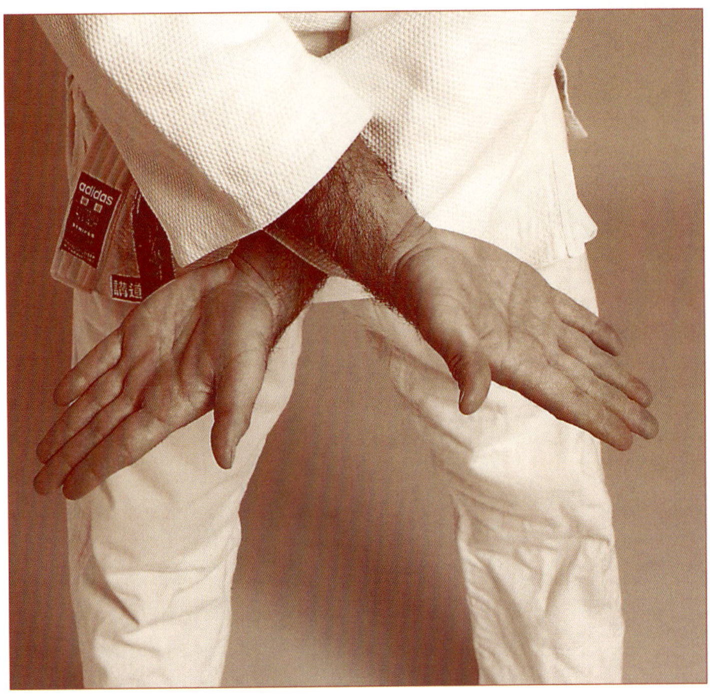

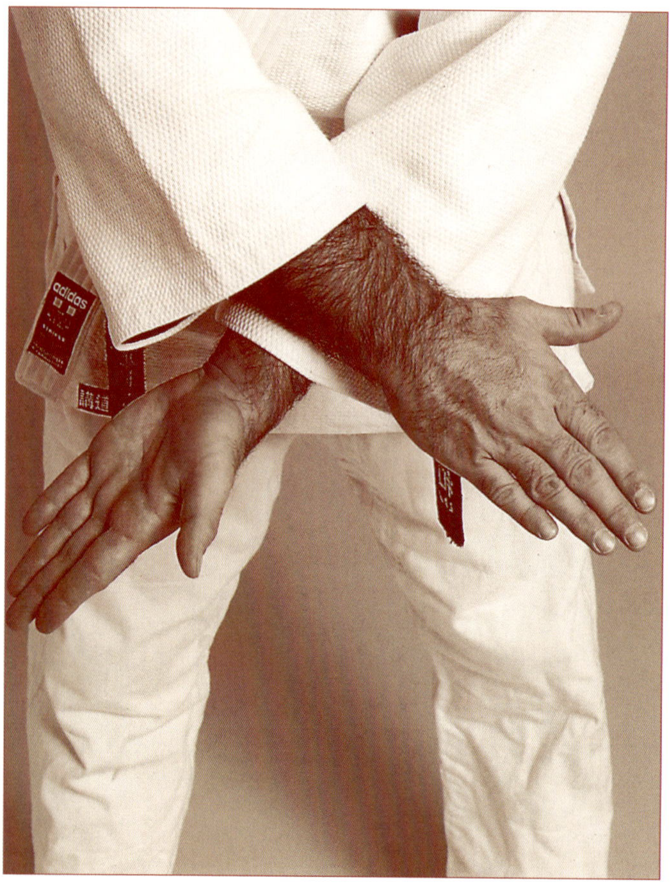

KATA JUJI JIME* (Half-Cross Choke)

Now the pressure is applied laterally to uke's neck. This time it's done with the pinkie of one hand and with the thumb of the other (the hands are crossed as shown in the image below, one in a natural position and the other flipped upside down).

HADAKA JIME* (Bare-Hand Choke)

The technique is performed from behind as the right forearm compresses the front of uke's neck; the left hand is over uke's shoulder with the palm facing upward, and the right tightly binds with the palm facing down.

OKURI ERI JIME* (Choke with Both Lapels)

This is performed from behind or from the side, with tori's right hand passing over the neck, grabbing uke's left lapel and, with the left hand, passing below uke's left armpit, grabbing the right lapel.

KATA HA JIME* (Single-Wing Choke)

This is performed from the side or from behind. Tori's right hand holds uke's left lapel and tori's left hand passes below uke's left armpit, pressing from behind the neck.

KATA TE JIME (Single-Hand Choke)

This is performed from the front or from another position. Tori grabs uke's left lapel with his left hand and makes a lever from the hold, compressing the forearm onto the neck.

RYO TE JIME (Double-Hand Choke)

Performed from the front with tori's hands, which hold the lapels of uke's judogi. Compressing the neck, tori turns the hold sideways.

SODEGURUMA JIME (Hand-Turning Choke)

Performed from the front or behind, with tori's right hand holding his own left sleeve, and the left hand holding his own right sleeve, with uke's neck between tori's compressing forearms.

TSUKKOMI JIME (Thrust Choke)

Performed in front as tori uses the right hand to hold uke's left lapel and left hand to grab the right lapel; tori pushes forcefully with the right hand in front of the neck and pulls with the left.

SANKAKU JIME (Triangle Leg Choke)

An arm should always be on the inside of the hold made by the legs.

DO JIME (Trunk Squeeze)

Performed from behind or from the front with tori's legs, which compresses uke's ribs and impedes uke's breathing.

This technique is not allowed in competition.

Third Group: Kansetsu Waza

Due to the danger of dislocation, fighters should use these techniques with extreme caution.

UDE GARAMI* (Arm Bend Lock)

With the left hand, tori holds uke's left wrist. With the right hand passing under the arm, tori holds his own left wrist; lifting the right forearm and maintaining a firm grip on uke's wrist, tori performs kansetsu waza.

UDE HISHIGI JUJI GATAME* (Cross-Arm Bar)

Holding uke's right arm, tori's left leg is placed across uke's chest with the foot on the other side of uke's head, and with the right leg below uke's right shoulder or over his chest. Tori must always push or pull in the direction of uke's pinkie, tighten the thighs, and lift the pelvis to accentuate the kansetsu waza.

UDE HISHIGI UDE GATAME* (Straight-Arm Lock)

Tori compresses uke's elbow toward tori's chest, helping with the legs, which press against uke's chest.

UDE HISHIGI HIZA GATAME* (Knee Arm Bar)

Grabbing uke's right arm, tori places the left knee on uke's right elbow, with the foot supported on the right side beside uke's belt and, controlling uke's left arm with the right, tori presses down.

UDE HISHIGI WAKI GATAME (Armpit Arm Lock)

Holding uke's left arm, which is in a prone position, tori supports the armpit on the triceps and forces uke's elbow with the help of the arms.

UDE HISHIGI HARA GATAME (Stomach Arm Bar)

Uke is on all fours; tori hooks uke's left arm with the left leg and places the foot behind the right knee. Tori arches the back and performs a hyperextension using the abdomen.

UDE HISHIGI ASHI GATAME (Leg Arm Bar)

Holding uke's left arm, tori places his left leg below and, pressing down, performs a hyperextension on the joint.

UDE HISHIGI TE GATAME (Hand Lock Arm Bar)

Tori holds uke's left arm with the right hand, passing below the arm and performing a hyperextension on the joint.

UDE HISHIGI SANKAKU GATAME (Triangle Arm Lock)

Tori is positioned in shime waza, but in this case, he holds uke's right arm and performs a hyperextension on the joint.

ASHI GARAMI* (Leg Lock)

This technique is not allowed in competition.

1. Uke is on his feet; tori bends the left knee around uke's right.

2. Tori forces uke to fall forward, pushing with the left leg and turning to the right over the side; tori performs *kansetsu* on uke's right knee.

Glossary

ayumi ashi A type of walking done with legs spread apart, alternating feet to travel closer to one's opponent. Not to be confused with tsugi ashi.

dan Literally "grades"; a ranking system used in many Japanese martial arts, including judo, in which levels are divided by experience and marked by belt colors.

densho Scrolls of instructions detailing advanced techniques awarded to high-ranking students of a martial arts discipline. Each densho is specific for each martial arts school.

dojo Literally "place of the way"; traditionally a place where students of Japanese martial arts went to train and study their discipline, although today the term is broad and connected to many physical training facilities in Japan.

happo no kuzushi Literally "destroy in eight directions"; the concept prevalent in many Japanese martial arts of unbalancing an opponent toward any of the eight directions surrounding a person at any one time.

hikite Literally "pulling hand"; the hand (usually on the non-dominant side) that grasps the opponent's sleeve area. Not to be confused with tsurite.

jigo hon tai One of the two most commonly used body positions in judo, performed defensively by placing both feet parallel to one another, about shoulder-length distance apart.

judogi The outfit worn by students of judo, consisting of a cotton, waist-length robe, ankle-length pants, and belt, the color of which depends on the athlete's experience and skill.

judo kodokan The official designation of the founding school of Judo developed by Jigoro Kano and established in 1882. Today the official headquarters of judo kodokan is the Kodokan Institute, an eight-story building in Tokyo, Japan.

judoka Athletes who study and practice judo.

kaeshi waza Any counter-technique used to deflect or mitigate an opponent's offensive technique. Ideally, the defensive technique will morph into an offensive technique.

kake Literally, "the powerful final execution of the throw or technique"; along with kuzushi and tsukuri, one of the building blocks of judo.

kata One of the principle ways of practicing and learning judo, in which an athlete follows a formal system of prearranged forms and exercises.

kenka yotsu An asymmetrical grip held by both opponents that leaves more space between the bodies than with other grips and thus makes it difficult for either athlete to effectively perform a technique against their opponent.

kihon Literally "basics" or "fundamentals"; a concept that covers all essential judo training, including form, breathing, stances, and offensive techniques.

kito, or kito ryu A fundamental school of jujutsu consisting of striking, throwing, joint locking, and choking techniques. This martial arts school would later provide the basis from which Jigoro Kano developed judo.

kumi kata Literally "grip form"; one of the fundamental aspects of judo, which determines whether an athlete can maintain balance while unbalancing their opponent.

kuzushi Literally "pull down" or "destroy""; one of the basic principles of judo, in which an athlete uses their own stability to compromise the balance of their opponent. An essential principle along with Tsukuri and Kake.

kyu A way of ranking the experience level of judo students, generally indicating a lower experience and skill level than dan.

obi The belt worn by the judoka, whose color is determined by the skill and experience level of the athlete.

ryu School or academy where martial arts disciplines are developed and taught.

samurai The old warrior class of Japan in the medieval and early-modern eras.

seiryoku zenyo The maximum efficient use of energy in both mind and body, central to the discipline of judo.

sensei Literally "before life," meaning "one who has preceded you"; any teacher of judo and other Japanese martial arts.

shisei Literally "posture" or "body position"; a fundamental concept of judo, which centers around the athlete's ability to apply the correct body posture to their movements to most efficiently throw their opponent.

shizen hon tai The starting position of judo, in which the athlete spreads their heels shoulder-length apart with feet pointing out, and distributes their weight evenly between the feet with knees and hips relaxed. This position allows the athlete to step freely forward and backward at any time while retaining the most balance possible.

tai sabaki The act of changing the position and direction of the body while maintaining a stable posture. There are three types of tai sabaki: *mae sabaki* (shifting forward toward the opponent), *ushiro sabaki* (shifting backward away from the opponent), and *mae-mawari* (shifting diagonally in front of the opponent).

tatami Textured floor mats used to practice judo, usually 6 feet by 3 feet (about 2 meters by 1 meter).

tori Literally "to take" and "to pick up"; the person who performs the actions during training exercises against their training partner (uke).

tsugi ashi A stepping pattern in judo in which the athlete advances one foot at a time, with the back leg trailing after the front leg, so the athlete's balance remains consistently in the leading leg. Not to be confused with ayumi ashi.

tsurite Literally "lifting hand"; the dominant hand of the athlete, which holds onto the lapel of the opponent and lifts when performing a *Waza* (technique). Not to be confused with hikite.

uke Literally "receiving body"; the person who, during training sessions, receives the techniques performed by their training partner (tori).

zarei Literally "seated bow"; a bow done sitting on the ground at the beginning and ending of each training session to establish respect between the sensei and judoka.

Further Reading

Books

Kano, Jigoro. *Kodokan Judo: The Essential Guide to Judo by Its Founder Jigoro Kano.* New York, NY: Kodansha USA, 2013.

McCall, Jeff. *Beginning Judo: The Ultimate Guide to Starting Judo.* CreateSpace Independent Publishing Platform, 2015.

Smith, Robert W. MA and Llyr Jones PhD. *Judo Kata: Practice, Competition, Purpose.* Santa Fe, NM: Via Media Publishing Company, 2016.

Websites

International Judo Federation

www.ijf.org

The official site for the International Judo Federation, featuring international rankings, lists of federations, and up-to-date judo news.

JudoSpace

www.judospace.com

A site offering online courses to judo athletes and coaches and contemporary research about the sport.

Kodokan Judo Institute

kodokanjudoinstitute.org/en

The official site for the Kodokan Judo Institute in Tokyo, featuring a history of the sport and information for beginners.

Index